Grayslake Area Public Library District
Grayslake, Illinois

1. A fine will be charged on each book which is not returned when it is due.

2. All injuries to books beyond reasonable wear and all losses shall be made good to the satisfaction of the Librarian.

3. Each borrower is held responsible for all books drawn on his card and for all fines accruing on the same.

DEMCO

MRS. SCROOGE

A Christmas Poem

CAROL ANN DUFFY

ILLUSTRATED BY BETH ADAMS

Simon & Schuster

New York London Toronto Sydney

Simon & Schuster
1230 Avenue of the Americas
New York, NY 10020

First Simon & Schuster hardcover edition November 2009

SIMON & SCHUSTER and colophon are registered trademarks
of Simon & Schuster, Inc.

For information about special discounts for bulk purchases,
please contact Simon & Schuster Special Sales at
1-866-506-1949 or business@simonandschuster.com.

The Simon & Schuster Speakers Bureau can bring authors
to your live event. For more information or to book an event
contact the Simon & Schuster Speakers Bureau at
1-866-248-3049 or visit our website at www.simonspeakers.com.

Design and spot illustrations by Nancy Singer

Manufactured in the United States of America

1   3   5   7   9   10   8   6   4   2

Library of Congress Cataloging-in-Publication Data

Duffy, Carol Ann.
Mrs. Scrooge : a Christmas poem / Carol Ann Duffy.
—1st Simon & Schuster hardcover ed.
            p.   cm.
1. Christmas—Poetry. I. Title.
PR6054.U38M77 2009
821'.914—dc22   2009034991

ISBN 978-1-4391-7633-7

For Barry and Tricia

with love

MRS. SCROOGE

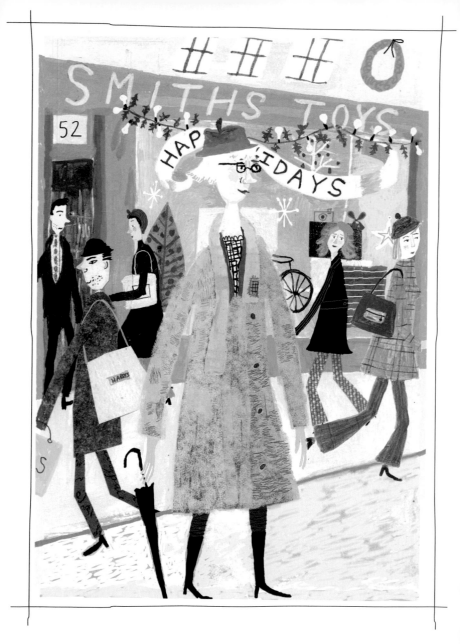

Scrooge doornail-dead, his widow, Mrs.
   Scrooge, lived by herself
in London Town. It was that time of year, the clocks
   long back,
when shops were window-dressed with unsold tinsel,
   trinkets, toys,
trivial pursuits, with sequinned dresses and designer suits,
with chocolates, glacé fruits and marzipan, with Barbie,
Action Man, with bubblebath and aftershave and
   shower gel;
the words *Noel* and *Season's Greetings* brightly mute
in neon lights. The city bells had only just chimed three,
but it was dusk already. It had not been light all day.

Mrs. Scrooge sat googling at her desk,

Catchit the cat
curled at her feet; snowflakes tumbling to the ground
below the window, where a robin perched,
pecking at seeds. *Most turkeys,*
bred for their meat, are kept in windowless barns,
with some containing over 20,000 birds. Turkeys
are removed from their crates and hung from shackles
by their legs in moving lines. A small fire crackled
in the grate. *Their heads are dragged under*
a water bath—electrically charged—before their necks
are cut. Mrs. Scrooge pressed *Print.*

She planned
to visit Marley's Supermarket *(Biggest Bargain Birds!)*
at four.

Outside, snowier yet, and cold! Piercing, searching,
   biting cold.
The cold gnawed noses just as dogs gnaw bones. It iced
the mobile phones pressed tight to ears.

                              The coldest

                              Christmas Eve

in years saw Mrs. Scrooge at Marley's, handing leaflets out.
The shoppers staggered past, weighed down with bags
or pushing trolleys crammed with breasts, legs, crowns,
   eggs,
sausages, giant stalks of brussels sprouts, carrots,
spuds, bouquets of broccoli, mangetout, courgettes, petit
pois, foie gras; with salmon, Stilton, pork pies, mince pies,
Christmas pudding, custard,
port, gin, sherry, whisky,
fizz and plonk,

all done on credit cards.
Most shook their head at Mrs. Scrooge,
irked by her cry "*Find out how turkeys really die!*"
or shoved her leaflet in the pockets of their coats, unread,
or laughed and called back "*Spoilsport! Ho! Ho! Ho!*"
Three hours went by like this.

                The snow

                        began to ease

as she walked home.

She hated waste, consumerism, Mrs. Scrooge, foraged

in the London parks for chestnuts, mushrooms,

   blackberries,

ate leftovers, recycled, mended, passed on, purchased

   secondhand,

turned the heating down and put on layers, walked

   everywhere,

drank tap-water, used public libraries, possessed a wind-

   up radio,

switched off lights, lit candles (darkness is cheap and

   Mrs. Scrooge

liked it) and would not spend *one penny* on a plastic bag.

She passed off-licences with *6 for 5,* bookshops with *3
   for 2,*
food stores with *Buy 1 get 1 free.*

                              Above her head,

the Christmas lights

                    danced like a river toward a sea
                    of dark.

The National Power Grid moaned, endangered, like a
   whale.

The Thames flowed on as Mrs. Scrooge proceeded on
    her way
towards her rooms.

                        Nobody lived in the building now
but her, and all the other flats were boarded up.
Whatever the developers had offered Mrs. Scrooge to
    move
could never be enough. She liked it where it was,
lurking in the corner of a yard, as though the house
had run there young, playing hide-and-seek,
and had forgotten the way out. She remembered
her first Christmas there with Scrooge,

                                    the single stripey
                                    sweet

he'd given her that year, and every year.
But Scrooge was dead, no doubt of that, so why,
her key turning the lock, did she see in the knocker
Scrooge's face? His face to the life, staring back at her
with living grey-green eyes and opening metal lips!
As Mrs. Scrooge looked fixedly at this,
it turned into a knocker once again.

8

Up the echoing stairs

to slippers, simple supper, candles, cocoa, cat,

went Mrs. Scrooge; not scared, but oddly comforted

at glimpsing Scrooge's knockered face.

But still, she double-locked the door, put on her
    dressing-gown

and sat down by the fire to sip her soup.

The fire

was very low indeed, not much on such a bitter night,

so soon enough she went to bed—night-cap, bed-socks,

Scrooge's old pyjamas, hot-water bottle, Catchit's purr . . .

and then her own soft snore.

She dreamed of Scrooge,

                    of Christmas past,

of Christmas present, Christmas yet to come; dreams

that seemed to trap her in a snowstorm bowl—

newly-married, ice-skating with Scrooge,

two necks in one long, bright red, woolly scarf;

or hanging baubles on the tree;

or being surprised by mistletoe, his kiss, the taste of
    him—

but then her world was shaken violently

and she was kneeling by a grave, hearing a funeral
    bell . . .

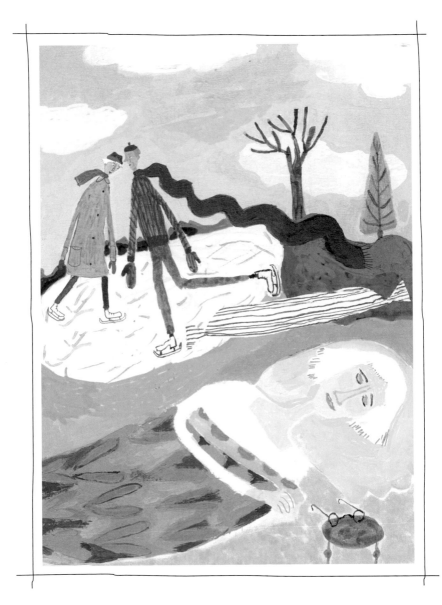

Midnight rang out from St. Paul's. She gasped awake.
The twice-locked door was open wide
and all the room was filled with light
and smelled of tangerines and cinnamon and wine.
A cheerful Ghost was perched and grinning on her bed,
now like a child, now like a wise old man,
with silver hair and berried holly for a crown
(and yet its shimmering dress was trimmed with
     flowers.)
"Good grief!" said Mrs. Scrooge, *"Who the hell are you?"*
The Ghost squealed with delight and clapped its hands
(a hard thing for a ghost to do, thought Mrs. Scrooge.)
"I am the Ghost of Christmas Past," it trilled,
"Now, rise! And walk with me."

It took her by the hand
then flew her through the bedroom wall. They stood at
  once
upon an open country road, with fields on either side.
The city had entirely gone, the darkness too;
it was a sparkling winter's day, all blinged with frost.
"I know this place!" cried Mrs. Scrooge. *"I grew up here!
We're near the village of Heath Row!
My family kept an orchard close to here."*
They walked along the road, Mrs. Scrooge recalling
every gate, and post, and tree.

"That way's Harmondsworth,"

she told the Ghost excitedly. *"Famous for Richard Cox,*
you know, who cultivated Cox's Orange Pippin."
The merry Ghost conjured an apple from the air.
She crunched delightedly. *"That way's Longford village;*
that way's the farm at Perry Oaks; and that way's Sipson
    Green!"
They'd reached the village now, a green, a row of houses
    and an Inn;
two fields away a farm, beyond that farm another farm;
the landscape glittering as if it were in love with light.
A laughing local bunch of lads ran by.
Mrs. Scrooge went red!
"I snogged that tall one once!" she said.

"They're shadows,"
said the Ghost, *"They have no consciousness of us."*
High in the sky there came an aeroplane, rare enough
to make the boys stand pointing at the endless,

generous air
and yell out *"Merry Christmas!"* to the plane.

"This is the

past,

it cannot come again," went on the Ghost, *"It is the gift*
your soul gives to your heart."

Mrs. Scrooge stopped in the road and turned. *"Why show me this?"* she asked. *"Because,"* the Ghost replied, *"Scrooge sends a message from the grave— keep going! You shall overcome!"* *"No Runway Three!"* cried Mrs. Scrooge, the breath her words made like a ghost itself, swooning, vanishing.

But when she
looked,

the face of Christmas Past bent down,
just like a lover stoops to steal a kiss,
and then her lips were soft, then salty,
tasting tears, her own, and then she woke,
at home, and old, and all alone.

Not quite alone,

for Catchit dozed and snuggled at her feet,

visions of robin redbreasts in his head.

London's moon,

the moon of Shakespeare, Dickens, Oscar, Virginia Woolf,

shone down on silent theatres, banks, hotels,

on palaces and doss-houses and parks,

on Mrs. Scrooge,

who lay, wide-eyed and fretful in the dark. She heard

a scrabbling noise inside the chimney-breast

and sat bolt upright in her bed—

"Who's there?" she said—

then, with a thump, a flash,

a figure in a crimson

Santa suit

glowed in the grate, as if the fire had taken human shape

and combed itself a beard from its smoke.

"I am the Ghost of Christmas Present,"

boomed the Ghost. *"Now rise, and come with me!"*

20

Before she knew it, Mrs. Scrooge sat in a sleigh,

being pulled by reindeers through the starry sky,

tying a ribbon round the earth;

the Ghost of Christmas Present talking as they flew,

    naming

the oceans, forests, mountain ranges far below,

until the Arctic Circle rose beneath them like a moon.

They landed,

          skidding on the ice,

in a percussion of sharp hooves and jingling bells.

Tears, like opals,

         fell, then froze,

on Mrs. Scrooge's cheeks as she looked.

She stood upon a continent of ice

which sparkled between sea and sky,

                        endless and dazzling,

as though the world kept all its treasure there;

                   a scale

which balanced poetry and prayer.

But then she heard a cracking, rumbling groan

and saw huge icebergs calving from the floe

into the sea;

then, further out, a polar bear, floating,

stranded,

on a raft of ice.

"The Polar Ice Cap melting," said

the Ghost,

"Can mankind save it?"

"Yes, we can!" cried Mrs. Scrooge. *"We must!"*

"I bring encouragement from Scrooge's dust," replied the

Ghost.

"Never give up. Don't think one ordinary human life

can make no difference—for it can!"

The reindeers steamed and snorted in the snow.

Mrs. Scrooge stretched out her hand to one,

stroking the warm, rough texture of its hide,

which seemed to alter, soften, into Catchit's fur!

The North Pole vanished like a snuffed-out flame.

She woke again.

"Old fool!"

said Mrs. Scrooge to herself, *"These are just dreams."*
She pulled her blankets up beneath her chin
and lay there, worrying about large things and small.
The wall flickered with strange shadows, shifting shapes—
a turkey, and then a bear, and then a hooded form
which pointed at her silently,
until it swelled and stood and spoke!
*"I am the Ghost of Christmas Yet to Come! Rise now,
and follow me!"*

It took her in its arms like a bride

and flew her through a winter wood

towards a clearing

and an open grave,

around which mourners stood,

then put her down.

"My family!" said Mrs. Scrooge. *"There's Bob!*

And that's his lovely wife!

There are my grandchildren! Peter! Martha! Tiny Tim!

Look! They're my dearest friends, the Fezziwigs! Their girls!

Why are we here? Who died?"

The Spirit pointed downward to the grave.

Mrs. Scrooge crept near and peeped into a wormy,

loamy hole.

She saw a cardboard coffin, crayoned brightly with a name,

cartooned with flowers, faces, animals,

covered with poems, kisses, hearts.

She turned . . .

At once, she stood beside the Ghost
inside a huge and crowded room,
her friends and family piling in!
In came a fiddler with a music-book
who started up a jig.

        (Mrs. Scrooge,

who loved a whirl,
restrained herself from dancing with the Ghost.)

In came Mrs. Fezziwig, one vast substantial smile,
bearing a tray of home-made, warm mince pies; saying
"She would have wanted it this way!" In came
the Fezziwig girls with babies chuckling in their arms.

    In came
tall nephews arm-in-arm with little aunts.

                            In came old
                            comrades

with whom she'd marched in protest
against every kind of harm.

                 In they all came,
aglow with life and possibility, old and young;
away they went, twenty couples all at once,
gay and straight, down the middle, up and round again,
the beaming fiddler trying to saw his instrument in half!

There never was
such a wake!

More dancing, then more music, someone sang,
several shed tears;
then mince pies, cake, mulled wine, cold beer,
more wine, more beer;
then Mrs. Scrooge heard a cheer
and there was Tiny Tim, up on a chair!
There was a hush.

"A toast!"

cried Tiny Tim, *"To my grandmother! The best woman
who ever was! She taught us all
to value everything!*

To give ourselves!

To live as if each day

was Christmas Day!"

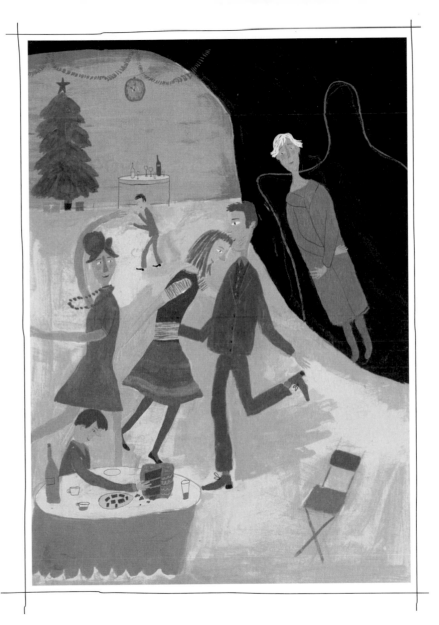

Another cheer and Mrs. Scrooge's name rang out
from everybody's lips.

She seemed to float
above them; all the bright, familiar faces

looking up,
raised glasses in the air.

She heard Bob say, *"She really had a wonderful life!"*

The Ghost of Christmas Yet to Come

pulled back

its hood.

She looked into its smiling, loving, grey-green eyes
and understood.

Clash, clang, hammer, ding, dong, bell!
Bell, dong, ding, hammer, clang, clash!
It was St. Paul's again,

gargling its morning bells,

the room her own;

and dribbling Catchit

staring down at her from her chest!
Quickly, Mrs. Scrooge showered and dressed.
She flung open the window and leaned out—
a clear, bright, jovial, cold and glorious day!
The doorbell rang.

Down she hurried,

opened wide the door,

and in they poured,

taking the stairs two at a time—Bob, Bob's wife,
the grandchildren, the Fezziwigs,
their girls, babies, partners,

all shouting

"Merry Christmas! Merry Christmas!
Merry Christmas!"

What news they had!

The credit crunch

had forced the property developers

to sell the empty flats below to the Fezziwig girls!

So, come New Year, all three were moving in!

Hurrah! Hurrah! What did Mrs. Scrooge think of *that!*

(And would she babysit?)

Bob came grinning from

the kitchen

with a tray of glasses of Buck's Fizz!

Mrs. Fezziwig and Mrs. Scrooge

cuddled and wept

with joy!

And that delightful boy, Tiny Tim, called out,

*"Here you are, Grandma, the sweet that Grandad gave you
every Christmas that he lived! A . . ."*

"HUMBUG!"

exclaimed Mrs. Scrooge!

"God Bless Us, Every One!" cried Tiny Tim.

⟨⟩ ABOUT THE AUTHOR ⟨⟩

Carol Ann Duffy is a poet, playwright, and freelance writer, and was made Britain's poet laureate in May 2009. She is the author of *The World's Wife, Feminine Gospels, Rapture,* and *New and Collected Poems for Children.* Duffy is a Professor of Contemporary Poetry as well as the Director of Creative Writing at the Manchester Metropolitan University. She lives in England.